Morgan's Birthday

Illustrations by Bill Slavin

First Novels

Formac Publishing Company Limited
Halifax, Nova Scotia

The development and pre-publication work on this project was
funded in part by the Canada/Nova Scotia Cooperation
Agreement on Cultural Development. Formac Publishing
Company Limited acknowledges the support of the Cultural
Affairs Section, Nova Scotia Department of Tourism and
Culture. We acknowledge the financial support of the
Government of Canada through the Book Publishing Industry
Development Program (BPIDP) for our publishing activities.

We acknowledge the support of the Canada Council for the Arts
for our publishing program.

National Library of Canada Cataloguing in Publication Data

Staunton, Ted, 1956-
    Morgan's bithday / Ted Staunton; illustrations by Bill
    Slavin.

(First novels; #21)
ISBN 0-88780-561-2 (bound) — ISBN 0-88780-560-4 (pbk.)

    I. Slavin, Bill II. Title. III. Series.

PS8587.T334M6725 2002	jC813'.54	C2002-901179-5
PZ7.S8076Mor 2002		

Formac Publishing
Company Limited
5502 Atlantic Street
Halifax, Nova Scotia B3H 1G4
www.formac.ca

Printed and bound in Canada

Distributed in the United States by:
Orca Book Publishers
P.O. Box 468 Custer, WA
USA 98240-0468

Distributed in the UK by:
Roundabout Books (a division
of Roundhouse Publishing Ltd.)
31 Oakdale Glen, Harrogate,
N Yorkshire HG1 2JY

Table of Contents

1
It's My Party

"WANTA COME TO MY
BIRTHDAY?" I shout to Ian.
It's indoor recess. Ian is busy
blowing a gum bubble into
Madeline's hair. It pops. Ian
picks some bubble out of his
nose.

"Sure, Morgan," he says.
"Cool."

"Great," I say. "Hey
Madeline, wanta come to my
birthday? We're going
bowling and mini-golf and the
zoo and a movie and go-cart
racing and a waterslide."

I don't know if we're doing

all of those things, but I want to.

"Thanks," says Madeline.

Guess what? My birthday's on Sunday and my party is Saturday. I'm kind of excited, which is why I'm bouncing up and down. Usually I only bounce if there's pizza, or chips or cake and ice cream. Hey, wait a sec, there will be. I bounce some more.

So far I've invited Charlie, Mark, Kaely, Lisa, Luke and Aretha, and now Ian and Madeline. Oh, and Zack, Rachel, Trevor and Robin. And Ben, Bobby, Will, Melissa and Heather. And — hey, soon I'll have invited my whole class. That's OK. There are only twenty-seven of them.

I bounce backwards from Madeline and thump, I bump into somebody.

"HEY," I yell, "WANTA COME TO MY BIRTHDAY?"

Then I turn around. Oh no. I'm looking at Aldeen Hummel, the Killer Godzilla of Grade Three, in her old purple sweatsuit. Her fist is up and her eyes are squinched behind her glasses, glaring. At me.

Did I say I'd invite my whole class? I was wrong. I wasn't going to invite Aldeen.

Except I think I just did. Aldeen blinks. She lowers her fist. I hear a strange little clicking noise.

"Oh," she says. Then, "Yeah, I guess," as if she's

doing me a favour.

I hear the clicking again. Aldeen turns. Ben is bending over her desk.

"Hands off!" she yells, and blammo, she nails him with an atomic wedgie, the worst I've ever seen. His pants are almost up to his ears.

Ben shouts. Our teacher comes scooting in from the hall. Aldeen looks at me.

"Do I gotta bring a present?" she says.

What have I done?

2
A Poached Egg

Inviting Aldeen takes away some of my bounce. Until, at supper, Mom and Dad say I can't have twenty-seven kids at my party.

"Awww," I say. Secretly I think, 'Good. Now Aldeen can't come. Bounce, bounce.'

"Twelve, tops," says Dad.

"I'm moving to Florida," says Mom.

She gives in when Dad says he'll run the games and do clean-up.

"No sweat," I tell him, "There's no clean-up at

bowling, mini-golf and go-carting."

"Morgan," Dad says, "I can't take twelve kids to all that. We'll have a party at the house. I'll take you and Charlie to one of those things on Friday night."

"Awwwwwwww." Really, I figure, Friday sounds good, and twelve is still lots of kids — and presents. It's just better not to say so.

"OK," Mom says, "But…" I hate buts. "I want you to invite Aldeen. She likes you, and I bet she doesn't get to go to many parties."

"AWWWWWWWWWWWW WW!" This time I mean it.

After supper, Charlie and I play Frisbee. Charlie's good

at it, but I'm not. So the way we play is Charlie throws, the Frisbee hits me; I throw, Charlie chases the Frisbee.

It doesn't matter. Mostly we talk about the party and Friday and how cool it will all be. I start feeling pretty bouncy again. I really whale the Frisbee. It whooshes down the street, the best throw of my life, except I was aiming the other way.

The Frisbee sails toward a kid on a bike. A kid in a purple sweatsuit. It's Aldeen.

"Look out!" I yell.

The Frisbee hits her. Aldeen hits her brakes. She looks at us, then scoops up the Frisbee and throws it into a tree. Then she rides over, her witchy hair bobbing. I remember Ben's wedgie. I feel like a poached egg disguised as me.

"Watch it, doofus," she growls at me. I hear the clicking noise. "I was coming to show you something, but forget it now." She wheels away. The noise goes too.

We start up the tree. Above me Charlie says, "Good thing she's not coming to your party."

"Oh yeah?" I puff. I look down and pretend my foot is stuck. I'm still feeling a little poached-eggy.

"Yeah, I remember her at Rachel's birthday in kinder-garten. She bit their cat."

I keep on pretending my foot is stuck. Really it feels as

if all of me is stuck — in a
birthday cake with Aldeen
Hummel sitting on the top.

3
Aldeen's Beans

My invitations say, "IT'S A MONSTER OF A PARTY!" There's a picture of monsters eating a cake. The purple one reminds me of Aldeen in a party dress. This is not good. When I hand them out at school, I'll save Aldeen's for last. I'm hoping maybe she's forgotten. Then I could skip inviting her and tell Mom that Aldeen said she couldn't come.

But no way. Next morning, Aldeen rockets over, trampling Kaely and Bobby on the way.

"Where's mine?" she says. Her hand is out. She's clicking again.

"Your what?" I say. I try to look mixed up. It's easy; I feel like I'm about to be put in a blender.

"My invitation. You said I was invited." Her eyes begin to squinch. It's a bad sign.

"Oh. Yeah. I forgot." I hand it over. It's a little bent from my pocket.

Aldeen looks at it for a long time. Then she says, "See what I got?"

She holds up a tiny box. Inside are four sandy-coloured lumps. Two of them are rocking back and forth, clicking against the plastic. Then a third clicks, and the fourth. They're moving all by themselves. For a second I forget about birthdays.

"Neeeat," I say, and they are. "What are they?"

"Mexican jumping beans," Aldeen says. "And know what? There's butterflies inside. If I keep them warm they're going to hatch and then I'll have pets."

"Wow," I say. We watch the beans going around. It's amazing.

"Where'd you get them?" I ask. "I want to get some."

Aldeen says, "You can't get them here. My dad sent them."

"Is he in Mexico?"

Aldeen says, "I don't know."

Aldeen puts the beans in

her pocket to keep them warm.

I remember my birthday again. I say, "Hey, Aldeen? Don't tell anybody you got invited to the party, OK? Because I couldn't ask everyone."

She stands her invitation right in the middle of her desk.

4
All Bummed Out

I'm eating my lunch — my favourite thing at school — when Luke asks, "Is Aldeen really coming to your party?"

"I dunno," I say. "My mom made me invite her. Maybe she won't come."

Mark scowls. "Last time I was at a birthday party with her, she tried to stick a hot dog up my nose."

"And remember at Janie's?" Zack shakes his head. "She made Ian eat all those chips and he barfed on the presents."

I didn't go to any of those

parties; I didn't live here then. I think I'm glad.

"Well, if she does come," Melissa says, "I can't. My parents said."

"Same with mine," Luke adds.

"Me too."

"Me three."

"But..." I say, "But, but — it's my birthday."

"Sorry, Morgan." Everybody shrugs and shakes their heads and eats their lunches. All at once, I'm not hungry anymore.

By supper time, it looks like not even I'll be going to my party — because there mightn't be one. Mom hangs up the phone after another call.

"That was Robin's mom,"

she says, "He can't come. Apparently Aldeen tried to flush his pet rat down the toilet at his party two years ago."

"Lauren isn't coming either," says Dad, walking in. "Aldeen punched Lauren's uncle when he tried to keep her from stealing the goody bags."

Oh man, I think, nobody's coming. On my birthday. No friends, no presents, no food, no fun: just me and Hummel the Bummel. How can she do this to me? Well, I know what to do to her.

"She can't come," I say.

"Of course she can," Mom says. "And she will. And so will your real friends, and we'll have a great time."

Yeah, right.

5
Mystery Girl

It's Friday afternoon. I'm a little bouncy and a little worried, like a ball without enough air. Tonight Dad is taking Charlie and me bowling and to a movie. That's the bouncy part. Tomorrow, Charlie, Trevor, Heather and Lisa are coming to my party. And Aldeen. That's the worried part.

Kids have found out about her beans and they start chanting at recess, like they used to.

Al-deen
Al-deen,
The great big purple
jumping bean.

Aldeen has a great big hairy
fit and throws Melissa's shoes
on the roof.

When she gets back from
being sent to the office, I'm
so worried about my party
that I forget to be afraid.

"Aldeen," I whisper, "If
you wreck my party
tomorrow, I'll..."

"You'll what?" She pushes
her glasses up with a grubby
finger and stares at me.

I become the Incredible
Shrinking Morgan.

"Never mind."

That night, Charlie and I

have tons of fun. Saturday morning I'm up way early. It's like Christmas. It's my party. I help put up streamers and balloons. I'm bouncier than they are. I help stuff goody bags. I wonder where the cake is.

Charlie, Heather, Trevor and Lisa show up at eleven, the way they're supposed to. "Happy Birthday," they say, the way you're supposed to. They have boxes and bags for me, the way they're supposed to. Some of them are big. I can hardly wait.

But I have to, because there's no Aldeen. She's late, late, late, the way you're not supposed to be. We hit balloons at each other and

jump on the couch.

"Maybe she's not coming," Heather says.

"Wouldn't it be nice," says Trevor.

There's a knock on the door. I open it and there's this girl. She's all dressed up in a sweater and a plaid kilt and knee socks and black shoes, as if she's going to church or something. Her hair is brushed and clipped back. She looks in and sees everyone and all the presents. She puts her hands behind her back.

"I'm here," she says.

Back in the living room, someone snickers. The girl glares. It's Aldeen, all right.

6
Picture This

Mom brings Aldeen in. We all stare. Nobody's ever seen her like this before. I notice for the first time that she has freckles. Aldeen stares back. She sits as if she's scared the chair will break.

Dad says it's time for presents. Everybody gathers round. I get a video game from Trevor, stomp rockets from Lisa, a space-station kit from Charlie and a bazooka water gun from Heather.

"Big deal," Aldeen mutters, and fidgets with her socks.

Then she says, "My present was too big to carry. It's going to be delivered tomorrow."

Even Charlie rolls his eyes. "Yeah, right," Lisa whispers. Aldeen starts to get her monster face.

Dad says, "Time for games. Let's go outside."

"She didn't even bring a present," I complain to Mom. "And she almost had a hairy fit. If she wrecks everything…"

I mean, this is my birthday. All Mom does is look at me as if I'm a TV commercial.

"Morgan," she says, "You'll live. Go out with your guests. I'm making lunch."

Outside, Dad has paper tacked to my play fort and squirt guns with water paint so we can paint pictures. He makes us put these big old shirts on to stay clean. Really that means we can squirt each other, so we do — except for Aldeen, who yells, "You better not!"

We were scared to anyway. But Dad says, "It's okay, Aldeen," and zap, he squirts her paint shirt with blue. Her mouth pops open, then, zip, she squirts green back. Pretty soon we're all painted, especially Aldeen. Everyone gets her. Maybe we get her too much, because finally she takes the green paint and dumps it on Charlie's head.

Then we play musical chairs. Aldeen wins, even though we all gang up on her,

because she gives murder noogies. When she wins, she sits in the chair with this grin on her painty face as if she's queen. Queen of Mean, maybe.

Then we get out my new water gun and the stomp rockets and try them. Then we climb up and down the play fort and run around and yell and play tag. Then Aldeen gets mad because everybody keeps tagging her, so she tries to hang Trevor off the play fort by his ankles.

Mom calls, "*Lunch!*"

7
Gross, Gross, Gross

We all go in to the table. The balloons and streamers are hanging down. There are funny napkins and party hats and paper plates. And food.

Except for presents, food is my favourite thing at birthday parties. There are hot dogs with ketchup, potato chips, pickles, pop, celery and carrots. Nobody touches the celery and carrots except Trevor. He sticks them up his nose and makes faces at Heather. Lisa doesn't eat chips so she throws a couple at Charlie. He hates pickles so he tosses pickle bits back at her.

I couldn't care less; I like everything. I want to chow down and get to the cake.

"C'mon, you guys," I say between bites.

"Yeahmf," says Aldeen. A little spray of hot dog bun comes out too. Her mouth is full. Aldeen hoovers food even faster than I do. How can she be so skinny and eat like that? I've never seen this before either. At lunch we always try to stay as far away from her as we can.

Now she's reaching for my chips.

"Owy!" I'm trying to say "Hey!" but my mouth is full.

I'd swat at her but I have a pickle in one hand and a hot dog in the other. She grabs a handful and tries to pour herself more pop at the same time. It spills. Aldeen shoves the chips in her mouth, then starts sucking up the pop on the table with her straw. How gross can you get, I think. I put more ketchup on my pickles.

Trevor starts coughing. Aldeen looks up long enough to pound him on the back. The carrot and celery shoot out his nose. "Eeeeewwwwww!" everybody says. Aldeen and I reach for the last hot dog at the same time.

"Hey! I got it first."

"Says you, fat boy!"

"Yeah, well it's my birth..."

Dad interrupts.

"Morgan, you've had more than enough. Come on, help clear the table."

I say, "I don't have to today. It's my birthday."

"I will," says Aldeen. She crams the hot dog in her mouth, jumps up and starts grabbing things.

"HEY!" Now the others are saying it.

"Shut up," Aldeen says, spitting the hot dog onto her plate. "You took too long. It's time for cake." Out she goes.

Well, I think, you can't argue with that. There's a crash in the kitchen. You can't argue with that either.

8
Taking the Cake

When we hear the crash, everybody looks up.

"Guess who?" Trevor snickers. He has the carrot back in his nose.

"She is soooo icky." Lisa settles her party hat. Pickle bits fall out of her hair.

"We should have painted her more," Heather says, "Like Morgan's dad did."

I'm starting to say, "I don't think that's why..." when, out in the kitchen, Mom starts. "Hmmmmmmmmmmmmmm."

It's the first note for "Happy Birthday."

And suddenly I don't care. This is it, the best part: cake time. Singing, candles, wishing, blowing, a corner piece of cake with extra icing, chocolate-chip peppermint-honey-crunch bubble-gum ice cream. Firsts. Seconds. Thirds, if no one's looking. I'm feeling so good that right now it doesn't even bug me that Aldeen is here. I'm bouncing in my chair. We've made it to cake. She can't wreck anything now.

Everyone is singing:
"Happy Birthday to you,
   Happy Birthday to you..."
And in comes Aldeen carrying my cake. It looks

like a triple-decker with chocolate-fudge frosting. There are white swirly bits in the corners. Oh yessssss. The candles are glowing. The light from them shines in Aldeen's glasses, which are tipping sideways off her nose. Mom is right behind, helping her along and carrying the ice cream.

"Happy Birthday dear Mor-gan," they sing, and Aldeen leans in. That's when her glasses slip, she jerks and a candle touches a balloon. BANG! Everyone jumps, and so does my cake. It sails up in the air, flips and lands in the middle of the table with a big fat, WHUMP.

9
Through at Two

There is one second of total silence.

Then I yell, "AL-DEEEN!!"

Aldeen screams and runs out of the room. Mom runs after her. Everyone seems to be shouting at once. Lisa is standing on her chair. Charlie is shaking his head. Heather is shaking a burnt candle. Trevor can't stop pointing and saying, "HO-LEEEE!"

"OK, OK," Dad calls. "Let's all sit down. It's no big deal."

Except it is too a big deal. Everybody is blabbing all

around me. For once I don't say a thing. I look at my upside-down cake. It's cracked and crumbling. All the good bits are mooshed into the table. Aldeen has finally wrecked my party, just the way everyone said she would.

Dad shovels hunks of cake onto plates and blops on the ice cream.

"It looks barfy," Heather says. She eats it though.

I am so bugged myself that I barely have two pieces. Lisa and Trevor are licking icing off the table when the doorbell rings. It's Lisa's mom, come to pick her up. Everybody but Dad is surprised that it's two o'clock already.

More parents arrive. Heather, Lisa and Trevor get their goody bags. They say thank you but they don't look very happy as they leave. What's their problem, I think. It wasn't their party that got wrecked.

"That was the best," Charlie says. Charlie is my best friend, so he's staying longer. His hair is green. He doesn't seem to care.

"See, when Aldeen started noogies, I thought Lisa was going to wet her pants."

I rub my head, remembering.

"Well, somebody shoulda noogied Aldeen."

"Where is she, anyway?" Charlie asks as my mom comes in. "Did she go?"

"She's in the backyard," Mom says. She puts a big piece of cake on a plate and hands it to me.

"I'm full for now," I say. Even I get full sometimes.

"It's not for you. It's for Aldeen. You're the one who's going to take it out there and apologize."

10
The Icing

"What?" I say. "She wrecked everything! Noogies, paint, no present, my cake..."

"She tried her best," Mom says. "And you wrecked her party."

"Her party!"

"Parties are for guests too. Now get out there and apologize."

Charlie waits in the living room. I shuffle outside. Aldeen is up in my play fort. She won't look at me. My mom does though. I don't get it but I don't have a choice.

I start climbing.

It's tricky with cake in one hand. As I get near Aldeen's foot, I wonder if she's going to kick me. She doesn't. She doesn't make room for me either.

From the ladder I say, "I brought your cake." She looks away and makes a long snork in her nose, the kind you make when you've been crying.

I say to her witchy hair, "My mom says I'm supposed to say sorry."

Snork.

"But, like, you know, when you go to birthday parties, you're supposed to be polite and not hit people and you're not supposed to drop the..."

She whirls around. "It was

an accident!" She has been crying. It's kind of scary. It's kind of sad too, I think. I get this squirmy feeling.

"I know," I say. "Sorry." That one just pops out, but it's OK. I mean it. "But, like, you're supposed to bring a present, too."

"I did bring a present but it was too little. Here."

She digs into her sock and pulls out a crumpled-up tissue. Inside are two little lumps rocking back and forth.

"Jumping beans," I breathe. "Cool. I thought you can't get them here."

"I don't need all of mine. These two are good jumpers."

"Oh wow." I look down in the yard. The rockets are

already broken. The video
game is boring. I have a squirt
gun. The beans and the space-
station kit are for sure the
coolest things I have gotten.
"Thanks, Aldeen."

Snork. "S'OK." She grabs
the cake and starts eating.

When she's done she hands me the plate.

"I want some more. With ice cream."

I start down the ladder.

Inside, Mom serves more cake. I decide I want some too. So does Charlie.

"Come see what Aldeen gave me," I tell him.

Charlie grabs his goody bag. We take the cake and the space kit out to the fort and climb everything up. Aldeen scrooches over to make room.

"What time do you have to go?" I ask her. "Can you stay for a while?"

"Oh, I told my mom not to come until supper," Aldeen says. She has icing on her glasses.

I start to say, "But the party ended at two." Then I decide to skip it.

Charlie says, "Hey, there's nothing in my goody bag but an eraser."

"That's OK," Aldeen says. "I've got tons of stuff."

For the first time I see everything from the goody bags piled in a corner. No wonder everybody looked unhappy.

"Guess what?" Aldeen says. "My birthday is next month. You're invited."

Two more new novels in the *First Novels Series:*

Robyn's Art Attack

Hazel Hutchins
Illustrated by Yvonne Cathcart
Robyn chooses the destination of the next class trip — the art gallery. None of her classmates think it's a good idea, not even her best friend Marie. But the art gallery surprises everyone, and sets Robyn's imagination soaring.

Lilly's Clever Puppy

Brenda Bellingham
Illustrated by Elizabeth Owen
Lilly gives her brother Mac a robot puppy, Bitsy, for his birthday. The other children tell him it's not a "real" dog. But when a friend's beagle gets stuck on thin ice, Bitsy shows what a robot puppy can do.

Look for these *First Novels*!

Meet Duff
Duff's Monkey Business
Duff the Giant Killer
Meet Jan
Jan's Awesome Party
Jan on the Trail
Jan and Patch
Jan's Big Bang
Meet Lilly
Lilly's Good Deed
Lilly to the Rescue
Meet Robyn
Robyn's Best Idea
Robyn Looks for Bears
Robyn's Want Ad
Shoot for the Moon, Robyn
Meet Morgan
Morgan's Secret
Morgan and the Money
Morgan Makes Magic
Great Play, Morgan
Meet Carrie
Carrie's Crowd
Go For It, Carrie
Carrie's Camping Adventure

Formac Publishing Company Limited
5502 Atlantic Street, Halifax, Nova Scotia B3H 1G4
Orders: 1-800-565-1975 Fax: (902) 425-0166
www.formac.ca